CLANCy
The Courageous Cow

Author's Note

I wrote and illustrated the first draft of this story for a school project when I was twelve years old. My teacher gave me nine out of ten. I think perhaps she took a mark off because I called Clancy a cow instead of a bull. Clancy is technically a bull—but he'll always be a cow to me!

Dedicated to all the cows out there

Clancy the Courageous Cow
Copyright © 2006 by Lachie Hume
First published in 2006 in Australia by Scholastic Australia.
First published in 2007 in the United States by Greenwillow Books.

Watercolors and graphite pencil were used to prepare the full-color art.
The text type is Jacoby Light.

Library of Congress Cataloging-in-Publication Data
Hume, Lachie.
Clancy the courageous cow / by Lachie Hume.
    p.   cm.
"Greenwillow Books."
Summary: Clancy the cow is a misfit in his herd, but when he proves
himself in the annual cow wrestling match, he demonstrates the foolishness
of judging by appearances.
ISBN-10: 0-06-117249-9 (trade bdg.) ISBN-13: 978-0-06-117249-6 (trade bdg.)
[1. Individuality—Fiction. 2. Prejudices—Fiction. 3. Cows—Fiction.] I. Title.
PZ7.H8883Cla 2007 [E]—dc 22 2006005591

First Edition 10 9 8 7 6 5 4 3 2 1

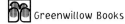 Greenwillow Books

CLANCy
The Courageous Cow

BY LACHIE HUME

 Greenwillow Books,
An Imprint of HarperCollinsPublishers

Clancy was born on a stormy day, a day
of great disappointment for his parents.
You see, they belonged to a herd of
Belted Galloways, but Clancy had no belt.

He was beltless.

As Clancy grew up, all the other cows treated him like an outcast.

Clancy tried hard to give himself a belt.
He rolled in the snow, but it soon melted off.

He tied a bandage around his middle,
but it gave him a tummyache.

He sprinkled sugar on his coat,
but the ants drove him crazy.

He even painted a white stripe around himself, but it washed off in the rain.

Clancy was different, and nothing could be done about it. Nevertheless, his parents loved him dearly.

The Belted Galloways lived on poor grass,
and they were all skinny. The field next to
them was full of rich grass and fat Herefords.

The Herefords held the grazing rights to their field since they'd won the Cow Wrestling Contest, which was held once a year.

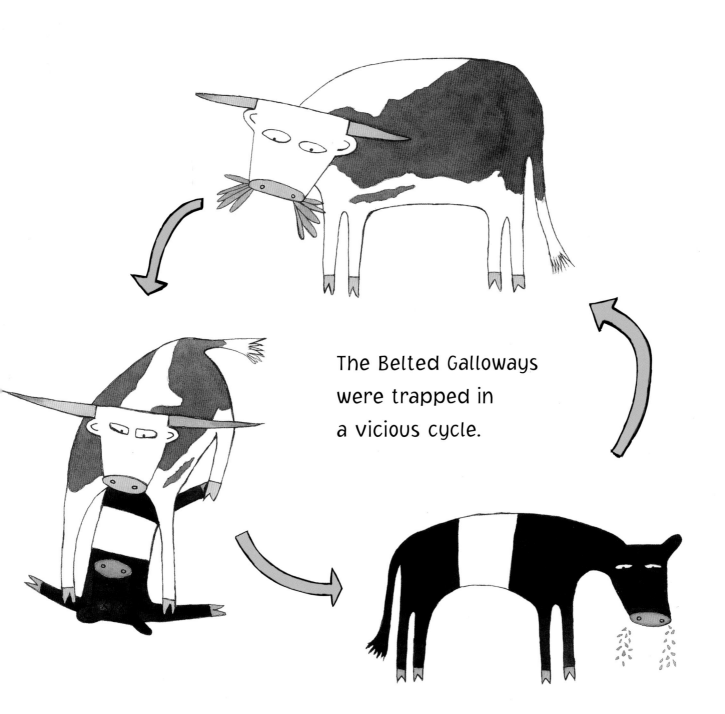

The Belted Galloways
were trapped in
a vicious cycle.

The Herefords grew big and strong on the rich grass,
so they always won the contest. This gave them the
grazing rights for yet another year.

Some nights the Belted Galloways tried to sneak into the Herefords' field to graze, but their white belts always glowed in the dark and gave them away.

One night Clancy slipped into the Herefords' field to try his luck, and nobody chased him out. He was invisible in the dark!

The next night, as Clancy grazed,
he bumped into another cow.
"Who is that?" asked Clancy.
"I am Helga," answered the cow.
"I am a totally brown Hereford."
Like Clancy, Helga had always been
picked on because she was different.

Clancy and Helga hit it off immediately,
and they grazed together every night.

At first only Clancy's mom and dad noticed how big he was getting.

Then one day he bumped into the president of the Belted Galloways and sent her flying! She started to bawl him out, then stopped in amazement. Clancy was enormous! Surely a cow as big as this could win the Cow Wrestling Contest!

The Very Important Belted Galloways decided that being beltless was not such a bad thing, and that Clancy would represent the herd at the Cow Wrestling Contest.

The Cud Cruncher

The Hindquarter Drop

Several retired wrestlers trained
Clancy and taught him their
favorite holds and maneuvers.

The Ruminator

The Helicowpter

The Cow Whisperer

The Windmill

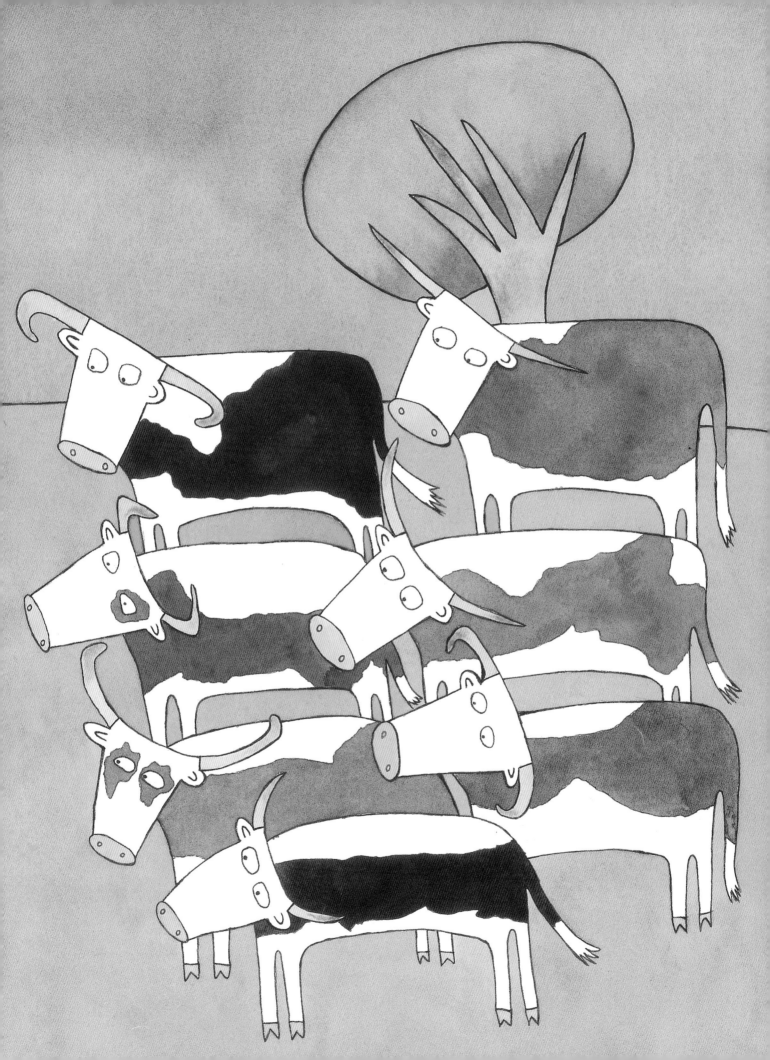

Now it was time for the Belted Galloways to enjoy the rich grass. They began to chase the Herefords out of the field.

Suddenly a voice rang out. It was Clancy.

Helga stood next to Clancy.
"This situation has gone on for too long,"
said Clancy. "Black, white, or brown,
we are all cows. I say we pull down
the fence and be cows together."

After a little while the Belted Galloways
and the Herefords began to get along
very well.

There was plenty of grass for everybody.